WALT DISNEY PRODUCTIONS
presents

Donald Duck's
Tallest Tale

Random House 🏠 **New York**

Book Club Edition

First American Edition. Copyright © 1980 by Walt Disney Productions. All rights reserved under International and Pan-American Copyright Conventions. Published in the United States by Random House, Inc., New York, and simultaneously in Canada by Random House of Canada Limited, Toronto. Originally published in Denmark as ANDERS AND SOM MESTERFOTOGRAF by Gutenberghus Bladene, Copenhagen. ISBN: 0-394-84740-7 (trade); 0-394-94740-1 (lib. bdg.) Manufactured in the United States of America

5 6 7 8 9 0   B C D E F G H I J K

Donald Duck liked to tell tall tales.

Donald and his friends talked about many things.

But Donald had to have the last word. About fishing, for example . . .

One day Donald, Mickey, and Goofy
went fishing.
They sat on the edge of the dock.

"This is great," said Goofy. "It reminds
me of the time I went fishing by myself.

"I felt a tug on my fishing line.
I started to reel the line in. Well!
What a fish! It was huge!!

"The fish dove under the water.
I almost went under, too. Finally, I
cut the line."

"That's nothing," said Donald. "Here is
my fishing story. I hooked a little fish.
Then a big fish came along.

"It was a swordfish. It snapped up my
little fish. It cut the fishing line.
It almost cut the boat in half! I was
lucky to get home alive!!"

That was one of Donald's tall tales!

Another day the
three friends went
on a picnic.

They drove out to the country.
They saw a nice spot under a big tree.

"A great place for a picnic," said
Donald.

"Moo," said a cow from the farm next door.
She thought the food looked good!

"Well," said Mickey, "that cow reminds me
of something.

"It reminds me of when I was out
collecting butterflies," said Mickey.
"Butterflies?" said Donald.

"Yes, Donald," said Mickey. "I chased one. But it led me right to a bull!

"I ran away very quickly!!

"I remembered what bullfighters do. I took off my jacket.

"I waved it around.
The bull kept trying
to run into the jacket.
But I made sure he
kept missing it.
Soon he got tired."

"How about the time I met a giant in the forest?" said Donald.

"The giant laughed when he saw me. He thought he could crush me with his foot.

"At first, I was scared.

"Then I walked right up to him.
I punched him in the knee.

"I knocked him over.
I hit him hard again.
Just like that!"

Mickey and Goofy
just smiled.
They did not believe
this tall tale.

Soon Donald decided to go on another trip.

He was taking his nephews, Huey, Dewey, and Louie, with him.

The nephews packed the car.

Donald carried his fine old camera.

"We are going to the desert," said Donald.
"We will have an adventure. We will look
for traces of ancient people and animals.
I will take pictures with my very special
camera."

Donald packed the
camera carefully.

Soon the whole car was packed.

They were off!

"Have a good trip!" called Mickey
and Goofy.

"I will come back with a good story,"
said Donald.

Mickey and Goofy laughed.

They had heard that before!

That afternoon they
arrived in the desert.
They saw the Mystery
Mesa.
"That's it!" cried Donald.

Mystery-
Mesa

"Mystery Mesa is where people and
animals lived long ago. It is a
large, steep rock with a flat top."

Donald parked the car.
He gave the orders.
The nephews unpacked the
car and set up the camp.

Soon the sun set.
It was bright orange.
Donald and his nephews
ate their picnic supper.
"We must wake up
early," said Donald.

The nephews fell asleep right away.
But not Donald!
He was too excited.
He was up at sunrise to climb the mesa.

Up, up, up
he climbed.

He rested on a
small ledge.
He did not see
anything ancient,
yet.

On he climbed.

At last Donald reached the top of the mesa.
The sun was hot up there.
Donald walked on, when . . .
SWOOSH! He slid into a hole.

Down he fell . . .

down . . . down . . . down!

He bounced
on his head.

Then he landed
with a crash!

When Donald looked around, he
was amazed.

The light on his hat lit up the walls.

"Wow," he said. "Look at the ancient
drawings on the walls. This discovery
will make me famous."

Donald took many pictures.

"Everyone will be proud of me," he said.

"I will win awards."

Soon he was ready to leave.
He looked around.
There was no other way out.
He had to climb out through
the hole he had fallen in.

He struggled to
get out.
Rocks kept slipping.

At the top, Donald
grabbed a branch.
He pulled himself up.
Stones and rocks
began to fall.
They blocked the tunnel.
"Whew!" said Donald.
"Now no one will be able
to see those drawings.
My photos will be the only
record. I will be a hero!"

At the bottom of the mesa Donald saw
Huey, Dewey, and Louie.

They were glad to see their uncle.

"Can we climb too?" they asked.

"Sorry, boys," said Donald. "But we
must hurry home."

Back home, Donald rushed to the camera shop.

"Develop this right away," he said.

He invited Mickey and Goofy to come over the next evening.

"The trip was great!" said Donald. "I discovered a cave with ancient drawings on the walls. People of long ago drew them."

"Wow!" said Mickey. "Will you take us there?"

"Sorry," said Donald. "I barely got out. As I got to the top of the tunnel, stones and rocks slid down and blocked it up. My pictures are the only record."

The nephews ran in just then.
They had the pictures.
Donald pulled them out quickly!

But what
was this?

"Oh, no," he said.
He looked at a few
more pictures.
"Oh, no," he said again.

Mickey grabbed the pictures.
"Look!" he said. "A picture
of Donald's hand."
Mickey started to laugh.

Donald was furious!

"All the pictures are of Donald's hand," said Goofy.

Donald had not held the camera correctly.

"Great pictures," said Mickey, grinning.
"Great story, too," said Goofy. "We can't top that one."
"But this time my story is true," said Donald. "It's true! It's true!!"

Goofy and Mickey laughed all the way home.
Maybe the story was true.
But they hoped Donald had learned a lesson!